www.hmhco.com
www.audreywood.com

The paintings were rendered in open acrylics on
stretched and grounded watercolor paper.
The text type was set in OPTI Adrift.
The hand-lettering was created by Leah Palmer Preiss.

Library of Congress Cataloging-in-Publication Data

Wood, Audrey.
The full moon at the napping house / Audrey Wood : Don Wood.
pages cm
Summary: In this cumulative tale, a chirping cricket calms a worried mouse,
a prowling cat, and other restless creatures, helping them to finally fall asleep.
ISBN 978-0-544-30832-9 (alk. paper)
[1. Sleep—Fiction. 2. Animals—Fiction.] I. Wood, Don, 1945— illustrator. II. Title.
PZ7.W846Ful 2015
[E]—dc23
2014038079

Manufactured in China
SCP 10 9 8 7 6 5 4 3 2 1
4500529005

For Rosalie Grace Heacock Thompson

There is a house,
a full-moon house,
where everyone is restless.

And in that house
there is a bed,
a wide-awake bed
in a full-moon house,
where everyone is restless.

And in that bed
there is a granny,
a sleepless granny
in a wide-awake bed
in a full-moon house,
where everyone is restless.

And with that granny
there is a child,
a fidgety child
with a sleepless granny
in a wide-awake bed
in a full-moon house,
where everyone is restless.

And with that child
there is a dog,
a playful dog
with a fidgety child
with a sleepless granny
in a wide-awake bed
in a full-moon house,
where everyone is restless.

And with that dog
there is a cat,
a prowling cat
with a playful dog
with a fidgety child
with a sleepless granny
in a wide-awake bed
in a full-moon house,
where everyone is restless.

And with that cat
there is a mouse,
a worried mouse
with a prowling cat
with a playful dog
with a fidgety child
with a sleepless granny
in a wide-awake bed
in a full-moon house,
where everyone is restless.

Until . . .

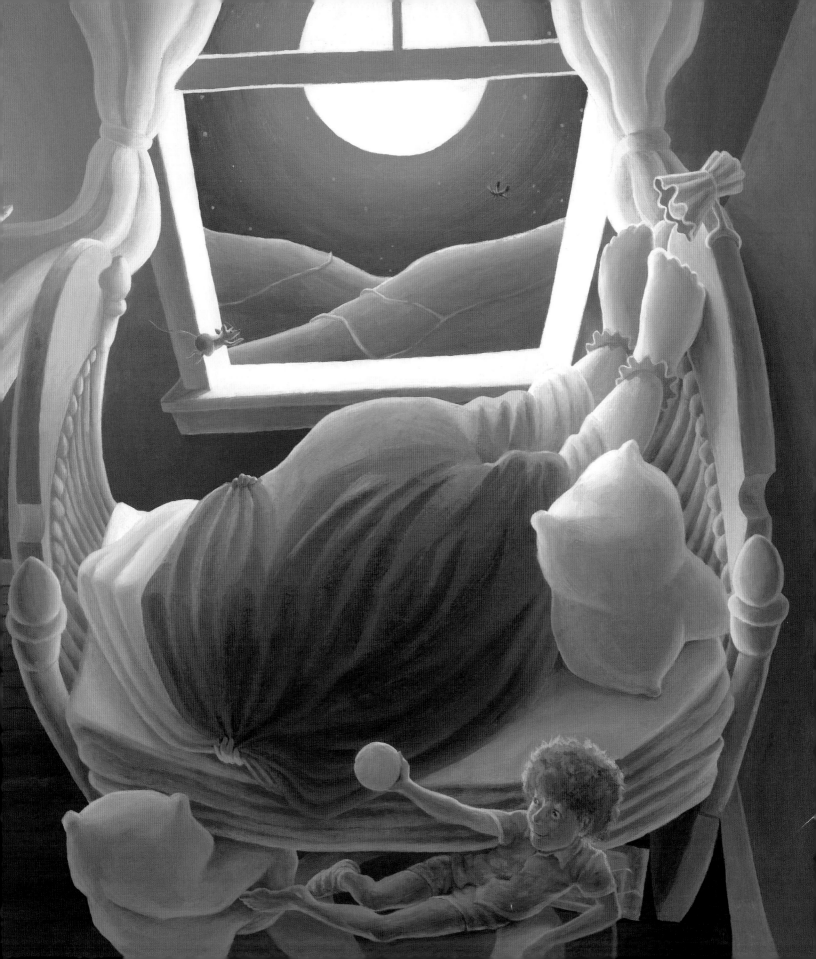

a chirping cricket
sings his song
to the worried mouse
and the prowling cat
and the playful dog
and the fidgety child
and the sleepless granny
in a wide-awake bed
in a full-moon house,
where everyone is restless.

A full-moon song
that soothes the mouse,

who calms the cat,

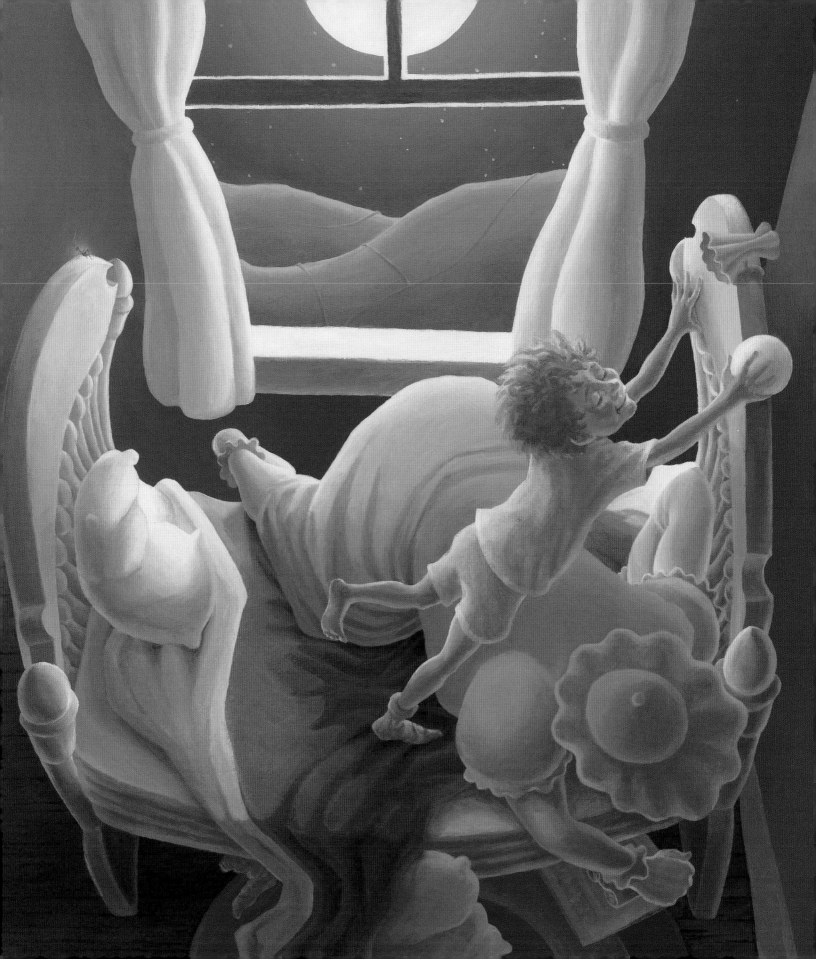

who gentles the dog,

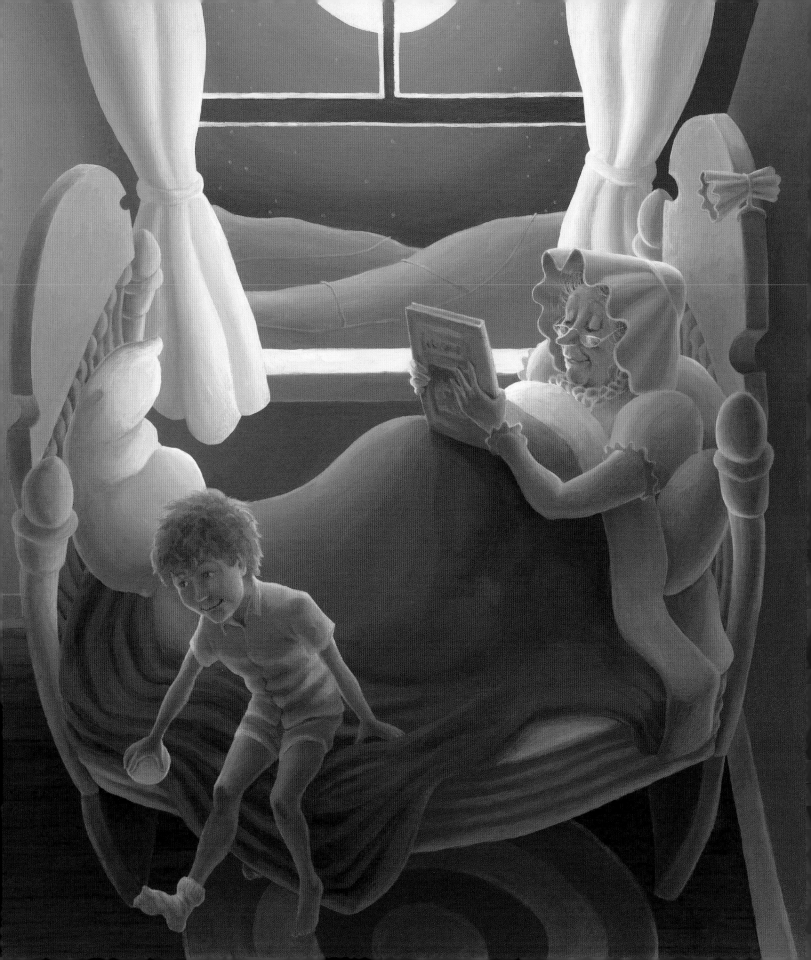

who snuggles the boy,

who hugs the granny,

in the dreamy bed,

He thought about working at Café Olé.

No . . . No . . . No!

He loved color and form and light and shadow, and he loved exploring ideas on his beautiful white canvases. Seymour Bleu, artist for all his days. If only he could figure out what to draw and paint.

Sadly he headed toward the Noble Fur Book Shoppe, hoping to find inspiration. There was something reassuring about the smell of fresh, colored inks on creamy new paper.

H e thumbed through emerald-green Bora Bora and flipped across centuries of lumbering dinosaurs. He browsed indigo-blue galaxies and drifted by sunken treasures in an azure mist. He visited studios of the old masters Leonardo da Vinci and Michelangelo, who were grinding pigments to bring frescoes to life and polishing exquisite figures released from blocks of Carrara marble.

Still no ideas of his own came. Still he didn't know what to draw and paint.

The art museum was his last resort. In the past he had always found stimulation and comfort as he strolled from gallery to gallery embracing the magic.

Racing through the sculpture garden and . . .

up the stairs to the museum entrance, Seymour Bleu was breathless when he barged through the steel-gray revolving door.

He zoomed from room

to room,

his hungry eyes darting from painting to painting, full of admiration. But for himself . . . he felt like a failure. He hadn't figured out what to draw and paint.

Dejected, Seymour Bleu walked up the street toward his studio and home. Ivory-black clouds hung ominously overhead and it started to rain, echoing the despair and emptiness he felt in his heart.

His studio
was dark except for
the single solemn cerise
light on his answering
machine. Not even
one call. Seymour
Bleu felt
depressed,
and alone,
and cold.

But as he began to make a fire in the little potbellied stove, Seymour Bleu heard the bells at the front gate jingle. Then the heavy, burnt-umber studio door burst open, and in marched his close friends, Bo Bo Steinmetz, Lady Foodles Fairfield, Oliver Gardener, and Simone Opoly (from Greece), each carrying a platter or bowl loaded with good things to eat.

The surprise on Seymour Bleu's face prompted Oliver Gardener to shout out, "What ho, Seymour Bleu! Have you forgotten about our dinner party? Didn't you make the leek stew?"

The feast was spread out on the table among the colors and the brushes and the tubes of paint. His good friends had prepared delicious dishes, all beautifully presented.

A sunbeam gilded Seymour Bleu's heart as his friends shared their bounty. Simone Opoly (from Greece) slipped her arm into his, with a squeeze. Late into the night the partiers ate and sang and laughed and talked.

Encouraged by the warm feelings he shared with his
guests and touched by their kindness, Seymour Bleu
remembered what inspired him most of all. And that
was drawing friends close to him.

That night Seymour Bleu
dreamed a vision for a
new series of
paintings.

At dawn he woke with great expectations
and leaped from bed in a delirium of
happiness.

From the pencil guided by his firm grip flowed a drawing onto the milk-white canvas—a map constructed to support his vision of color.

Seymour Bleu sashayed across the floor, picked up his paintbrush, and

began to paint.

Seymour Bleu's Color Mixing Tips:

yellow + red = orange
red + blue = purple
blue + yellow = green

You can create any color by
combining the three primary colors—
yellow, red, and blue—in different ways.
Some of my favorite combos are:

more blue + less yellow = a sea-green wave
less blue + more yellow = a chartreuse lizard